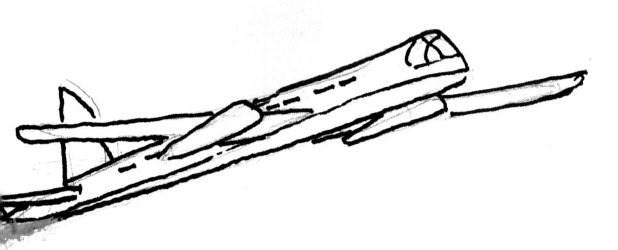

Papa flew to the North Pole to spend the night with HIS BUDDY. They enjoyed a cup of hot chocolate by the fire.

"Santa, I want to go see Dasher, Dancer, Prancer, Vixen, Comet, Cupid, Donner, Blitzen and Rudolph—the most famous reindeer in the whole world!!"

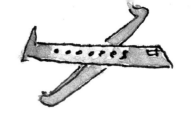

And Santa, "Can the reindeer
take you and me for a ride?"
"Sure," said Santa.

Papa said, "Santa,
we are flying as high as
the airplanes."

The next morning, Mrs. Claus
fixed a BIG breakfast.

Papa said, "Mrs. Claus, you are the best cook in the world! If I stayed too long, I would be as FAT as Santa..."
We all had a good laugh.

Papa said,
"Santa, all my babies love donuts!"
Santa asked, "Why is that?"

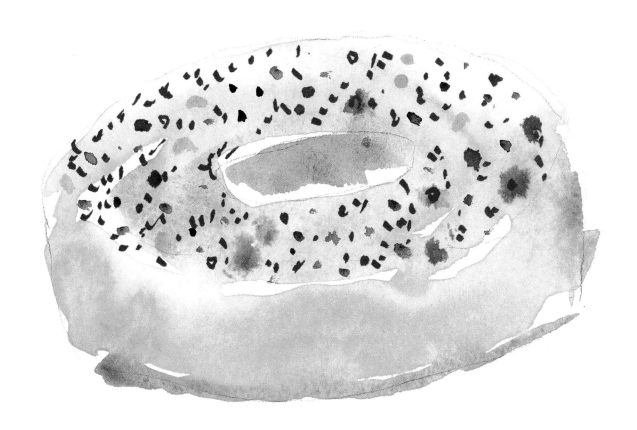

Papa answered, "Because they taste SO, SO GOOD AND THEY MAKE YOU STRONG."

Papa said, "When I see that
HOT SIGN,
I get so excited! I can't hold my car back
from going straight for the donuts."

Papa said, "Krispy Kreme's are SO good
I brought you FOUR boxes.
Now, don't let Mrs. Claus, Rudolph
or the Elves have any.
These are for my buddy."

Papa said, "I wish you could help me
make a Donut Tree for my babies."

Santa said, "That's a great idea!
Why don't we go to the workshop
and get all the Elves working on it!"

Santa had 1,000 ELVES
in his giant workshop
making toys for all the
girls and boys.

Santa said to all the elves,
"Papa, MY BEST BUDDY,
wants to make a Donut Tree
for ALL HIS BABIES."

13

Santa said, "This is your number one job, STOP WORKING on all the toys for Christmas! I have a special job for you!!"

"OK, let's get to work and learn how to grow a Donut Tree." One of the elves said, "First we have to make a Donut Tree Seed like an Apple Tree Seed and an Orange Tree Seed."

The elves ran to Santa and Papa and said,
"WE GOT IT!!! WE GOT IT!!!"

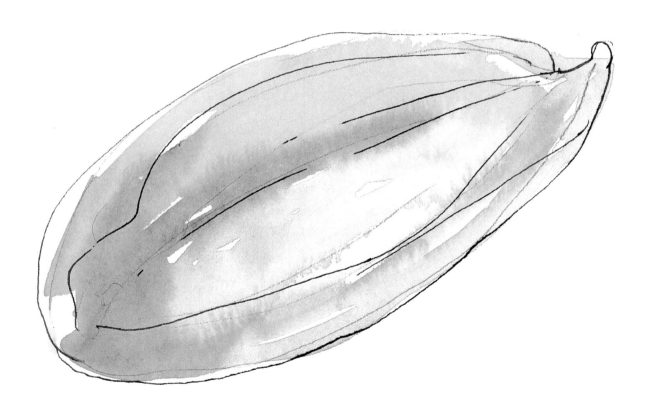

Papa said, "BIG PROBLEM,
my babies like different kinds of donuts—
PLAIN, CHOCOLATE, SPRINKLES AND PINK.
So it would have to be a MAGIC DONUT SEED."
Santa said, "Ok, let's get to work
and make A MAGIC DONUT SEED."

The elves were so excited—
"WE DID IT! WE DID IT!
The magic seed grows all kinds of
donuts—PLAIN, CHOCOLATE,
SPRINKLES, PINK AND SURPRISES!"

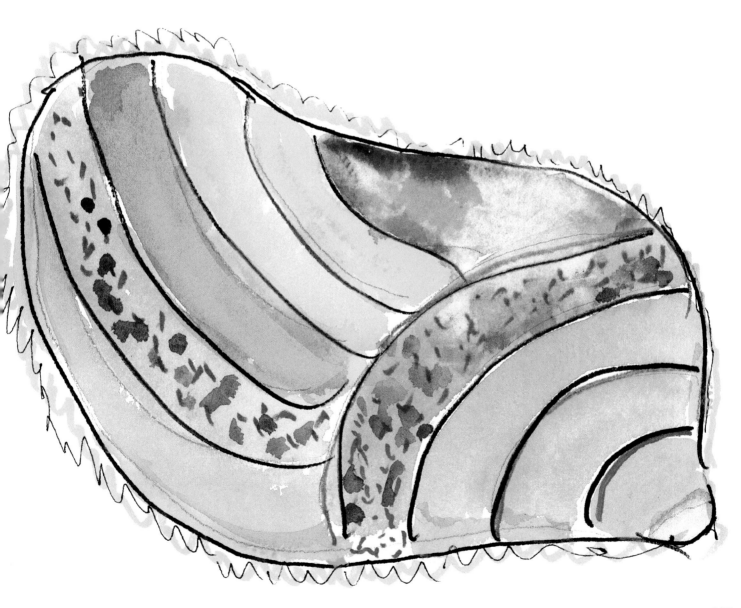

So Papa flew
back to Palm
Beach with the
Magic Donut
Seed and
planted it.

18

Every day the
Donut Tree grew,
bigger and
bigger.

1 mo. 2 mo. 3 mo. 4 mo. 6 mo. 8 mo. 12 mo.

Look at all the
different donuts.

"Kids, let's take a picture of the Donut Tree and send to my buddy, Santa."

"Don't you think we should write a letter thanking Santa and the Elves for our Donut Tree?"

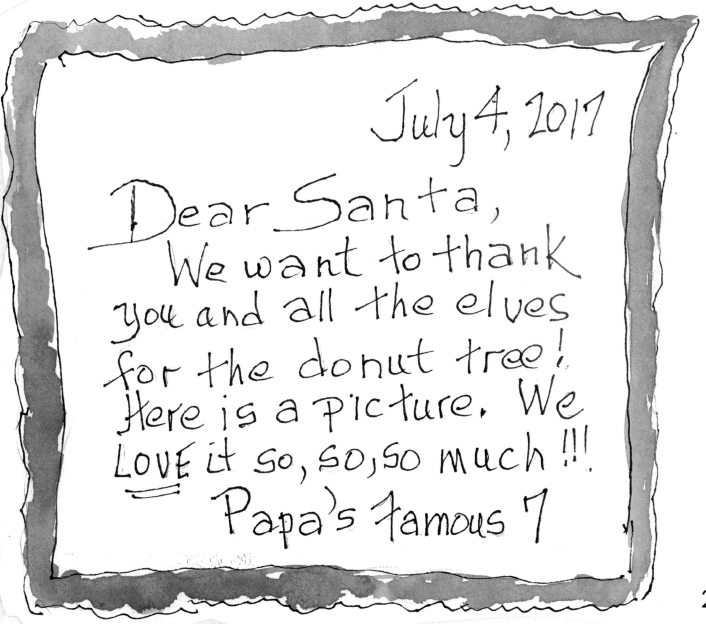

July 4, 2017

Dear Santa,
We want to thank you and all the elves for the donut tree! Here is a picture. We LOVE it so, so, so much !!!
Papa's famous 7

Papa said, "Now that we have a Donut Tree, you can eat donuts all day..."

- WHEN YOU WAKE UP
- DURING THE DAY
- BEFORE YOU GO TO BED

All the babies said,
"PAPA, YOU ARE THE BEST PAPA
IN THE WHOLE WORLD AND WE LOVE
YOU UP TO THE SKY..."

Papa said, "Now remember—
don't tell THE OLD PEOPLE.
You can eat, and eat, and eat some more."

Georgia   Maddie   Allie

Andrew   Liz   Maddie

Arthur

THE END

Dedicated to my seven "babies":

Liz

Arthur

Allie

Andy

George

Mookie

MaaMaa

The most perfect grandchildren
God ever made.

Made in the USA
Monee, IL
21 September 2021